good deed rain

46 Books by Allen Frost

...Ohio Trio...Bowl of Water...
...Another Life...Home Recordings...
...The Mermaid Translation...The Selected
Correspondence of Kenneth Patchen...
...The Wonderful Stupid Man...
...Saint Lemonade...Playground...Roosevelt...
...5 Novels...The Sylvan Moore Show...
...Town in a Cloud...A Flutter of Birds
Passing Through Heaven: A Tribute to Robert
Sund.......At the Edge of America.......
....Lake Erie Submarine....The Book of Ticks....
.........I Can Only Imagine.........
...The Orphanage of Abandoned Teenagers...
...Different Planet...Go With the Flow: A
Tribute to Clyde Sanborn...Homeless Sutra...
..The Lake Walker..A Hundred Dreams Ago..
....Almost Animals....The Robotic Age....
....Kennedy....Fable....Elbows & Knees:
Essays and Plays....The Last Paper Stars....
...Walt Amherst is Awake...When You Smile
You Let in Light....Pinocchio in America....
....Florida....Blue Anthem Wailing....
...The Welfare Office...Island Air...
...Imaginary Someone...Violet of the Silent
Movies....The Tin Can Telephone....
....Heaven Crayon....Old Salt....
...A Field of Cabbages...River Road...
....The Puttering Marvel....
...Something Bright...

SOMETHING BRIGHT

SOMETHING BRIGHT © 2021
Allen Frost, Good Deed Rain
Bellingham, Washington
ISBN 978-1-63901-713-3

Writing & Drawings: Allen Frost
Cover Photograph: Rustle Frost
Cover Production: Katrina Svoboda
Back Cover Acclamation: Jason Graham
Apple: TFK!

Credit:
The Collected Songs of Cold Mountain, Translated by Red Pine, Copper Canyon Press, 2000.
"Brass Foot" from *A Parent's Guide to Raising Piranha*, 2004.
"Lucky" from *The End of Beryllium*, 1997.

> *find a magic melon in your dreams*
> *steal a sacred orange from the palace*
> *far away from your native land*
> *swim with fish in a stream*
>
> —Cold Mountain

SOMETHING BRIGHT

Allen Frost

Good Deed Rain ◊ Bellingham, Washington ◊ 2021

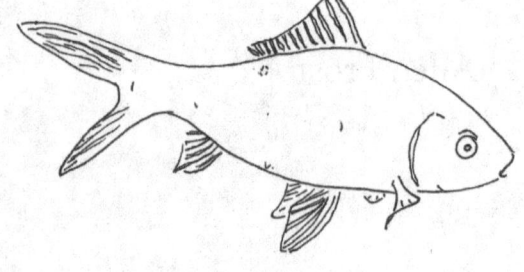

the chapters

1944	17
God Bless You Too	18
Jake the Dog	19
The End of Johnson Dracula	20
Meeting Harpo	21
Myrna Loy	22
Missing Miles	23
The Great Beyond	24
The Pond Ballet	26
The Bird Book Migration	27
The Smoke	28
The Martian Mailman	29
The Human Cannonball	30
A Rare Sight on a Winter Day	31

Bert from Montana	32
The Dogcatcher's Ghost	33
Leaving this World Through a Pool of Water	34
The Orange Horse	35
The Trees of Mayhew Park	36
Apparently a Bird	37
Brass Foot	38
Lucky	39
The Lake Erie High School Marching Band	40
Bring Out Barbara	41
Church Music	42
The Bright Puddle	43
The Coin Factory	44
The Laugh Track	47
The Hidden River	48
1962	49
The Alligator Bank	51
Life in the Innertube	52
The Author of Water	53
The Neighbors	54
Asleep in Ohio	55
Dream Telegram	57
The Cows of 32nd Street	58

The Mermaid Next Door	60
The Robot	61
A Gallon of Milk	62
Something to Talk About	63
The Field	64
The Chickens	65
4 Birds	66
The Visible Woman	67
Among the Seagulls	68
The Voice of the Sea	69
Something Bright	70
The Forest of the Moon	71
Her Little Farm	72
Inside	73
Snow Hotel	74
A Classic	76
The Ash	77
The Right Conditions	78
The Beginning	79
Puzzles	80
The Shell	81
A Red Letter Day	82
The World Series in Heaven	83

A Bite of Apple	84
A Moment with the Map	85
The Amalgamated Transit Union	86
Betty's Dog	88
When I was Superman	89
A House on a Street Full of Stars	90
The Deer Tailor	91
Karen Wagner's Dog	92
King in a Taxi	93
The Orson Welles Cinema	94
1911	95
The Snow Pharaoh	96
Just Married	98
The 24th Street River	99
The Martian Mailman Returns	100
The Frequency of Other Worlds	101
Ohio Fairy Tale, part 1	102
Ohio Fairy Tale, part 2	103
Comfort	104
Miss Millipede	105
10,000 Spring Flowers	106
A Victim of Helium	107
A Cup of Sugar	108

The Farmers' Almanac Predicts 109
A Distant Bark 110
Vienna Cuckoo Clock Cleaners 111
A Blue Octopus 112
The Friendly Giant 113
1973 114
The Sea Visitor, part 1 115
The Sea Visitor, part 2 116
The Sea Visitor, part 3 117
1934 118
Rhubarb Radio 119
The Other House 120
Underground and in the Wind 121
Rooster Fish 122
An Astronaut Parade 123
A Better, More Peaceful World 124
The Invisible Woman 125
The Dream Bird 126
The Tricycle Miracle 127
Before Words 128
Crabgrass 129
Spring Equinox 130
The One with the Picket Fence Smile 131

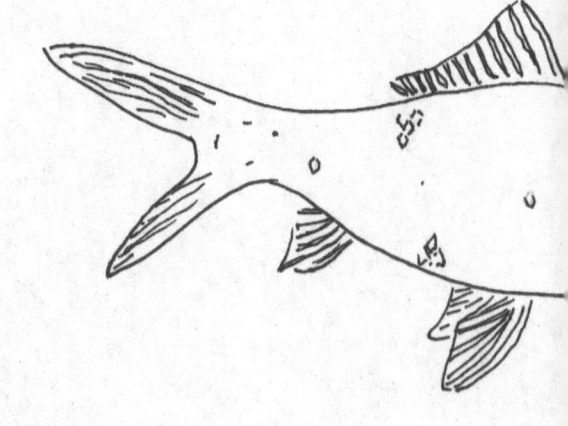

1944

Wallace Beery is walking around a bus station. Lots of soldiers. He doesn't know if he's in the right place or not but he's willing to find out.

GOD BLESS YOU TOO

As a prayer, I was reading *God Bless You, Mr. Rosewater* on a little propeller airplane that was folding above New England like origami. I have the sky to thank for not crumpling me up. I carried that blue paperback around with me a lot after that. At the Grand Illusion café, my friend and I pretended we saw Kurt Vonnegut at the other table. There was no way that was him, it was laughable of course, but it was fun to imagine. We looked forward to their coffee but if he wasn't there, we would miss him terribly.

JAKE the DOG

I saw his owner at the corner store coming from the back by the cooler. "I sure miss that dog," he said. Me too, I told him. What else can you do when someone is sad? Then I remembered the scene that windy early morning a year ago. Friday is garbage day when barrels and bins are set out on the curb and I watched Jake from a distance. The wind had blown everything over, littering the sidewalk and street. It was heaven for a dog—between his paws he had a tin can, sipping it like nectar.

The END of JOHNSON DRACULA

A vampire's death never comes easy. But in every movie, they seem to go the same way—caught in the cross of a chapel window shadow, falling off a balcony onto something jagged below, or someone just plain pounds the life out of them with a stake through their chest. Johnson Dracula was no different. When it was his time, he was in a rocking chair. He never saw it coming. The moon made the crickets go like radio. He was mesmerized by the creak of the rockers. Then it happened. The chair broke, and as he fell to the floor, a snapped piece went right into his heart and that was it.

MEETING HARPO

One night in New York City, I was at the infamous Blue & Gold which had a pool table downstairs, watching someone play. All of a sudden, the steps clattered with Harpo Marx descending on roller skates! (You could say it was someone perfectly dressed as him, raincoat and top hat, yellow wig and horn, but the apparition was so out of the blue and wonderful I know it was really him). He slid up to the startled guy playing, grabbed the cue stick and took a quick shot at a ball and before anyone could say a word, he clunked back up the steps and zoomed away. This really happened! The world is more beautifully mysterious than meets the eye.

MYRNA LOY

He thought about Myrna Loy. She lived a long time ago. She only existed in silver, charcoal, white, like a girl in an oyster shell. Sometimes she would appear in his TV and he would watch her every move. If only she would take his arm, the city would be their scenery.

MISSING MILES

I had a chance to see Miles Davis: a ticket, a ride to New York City, a place to stay the night. All I had to do was say yes. Who cared if I was in school with classes and essays due? Why didn't I know what I do now? I held a warm cup of coffee and thought of that long cold winter drive down from Maine. It can take years to find that road.

The GREAT BEYOND

Past the ring toss and the shooting gallery, around the tent, mind the ropes staked to the trampled ground. A painted wooden carriage, the door is open, she sits at a table in the candlelight. She can read the lines of your hand and see your future. She has gathered advice from the Great Beyond. But take it with a grain of salt—after you pay, she is the first to admit, "What do I know? I live in a circus."

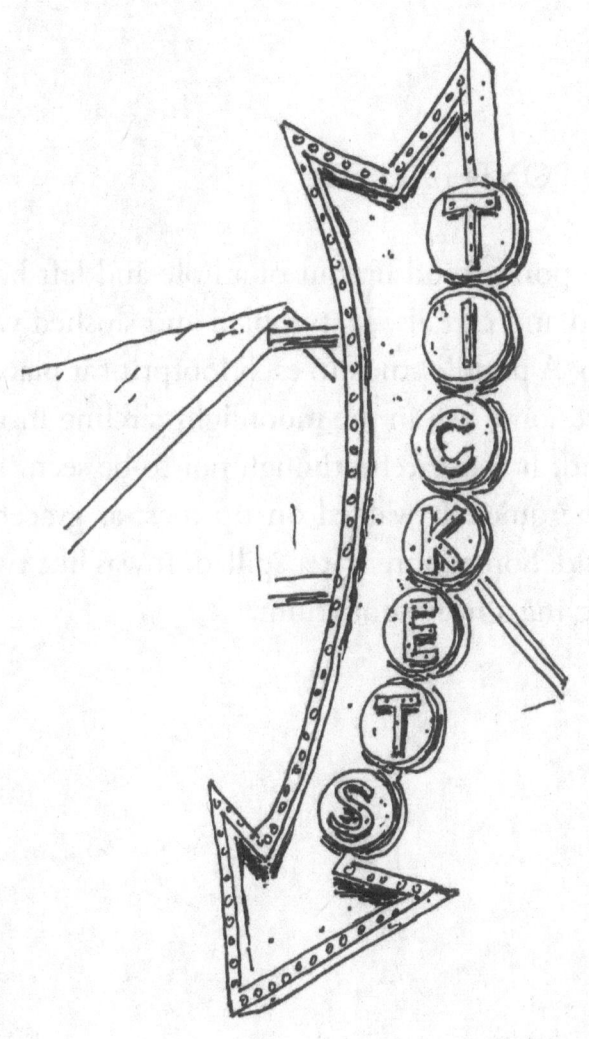

The POND BALLET

The pond stood up out of a hole and left behind the mud and cattails. It stumbled and sloshed with every step. A puddle stuck to each footprint it placed. There were some fish in the moonlight circling inside of the pond. It was careful though not to be seen. It wanted to be quiet. It walked on tip toes, as gracefully as it could. Some more water spilled. It was like two people carrying a heavy aquarium.

The BIRD BOOK MIGRATION

Every year at this time, the bird book hops to the edge of the shelf, opens its covers as wings and flaps around the room wildly. It stirs the curtains as it bumps against the window. The gray sky is beckoning. I hold it carefully and bring it to the door. I know I won't see it for a while. Way past the telephone wires, up above town, a formation circles.

The SMOKE

Uncle Charlie was sent to a wet airfield in England during World War Two. He would wait for the bombers coming back from burning Germany. He would watch the gray sky and to ease the time he would add smoke to the air. He picked up the habit of smoking a pipe while he was stationed there.
Think of those wounded fliers watching the water, then land flashes beneath the rips in their plane. They just wanted to be back on the ground, the blurring trees and green fields. If it would just hold them down, they promised they would never leave. The smoke followed him home across the sea, a tin of tobacco, a pipe rack with chestnut colors smooth as racehorses. We would watch him leaned back in his chair and remember the way his face looked as he smoked.

The MARTIAN MAILMAN

Black night sky. Some orange lights flash from a little white truck, dented like a box of crackers. It is stopped beside a mailbox planted by the dusty road. This is the first one in miles, driving past the ghostly weeds, caught in the dim headlights. The engine idles, skips and grumbles, coughs rust. The squeak of the latch. The Martian mailman leaves a letter in each box he gets to, a limited-time-only insurance offer from a distant planet Earth.

The HUMAN CANNONBALL

I only knew him as an old man, after his circus days were long gone. When I visited him at his little acre by the pond, he would tell me stories and show me pictures and on sunny days we would go out to the field. He kept the cannon under tarps and ever so gingerly he would crawl inside. When he gave the word, I would light the fuse and I would hold my ears and watch for a glimpse of him going by in the sky.

A RARE SIGHT on a WINTER DAY

Three butterflies gather around a cigarette someone left on the sidewalk. It's cold enough they need to wear their winter coats, scarves and hats. They hold their hands to the heat and stamp their feet and one of them says something, a word that makes a cloud so miniscule you need a microscope to see.

BERT from MONTANA

He would arrive in the summer in a big white station wagon that had rolled 1000 miles. We'd be on the sidewalk, ready to start all over. For me it was always imaginary, for Bert it was talk. Even at 10, he was already talking like a salesman, telling us how things were done in Montana and how Seattle had a lot to learn. He took over whenever he got out of that Chevrolet and all I could do was play along.

The DOGCATCHER'S GHOST

Now he spends his days invisible to us, but if you listen hard you might hear him as he crosses fields and streets, net in hand, spooning out apologies.

LEAVING this WORLD THROUGH a POOL of WATER

A few days before our dog died, I started digging a hole in the backyard. She let us know it was her time and her spirit had been slowly floating towards that space surrounded by blackberry, bamboo, and a slender willow tree. The trouble is: it has been raining solidly since Saturday. The grave became a pond. I had to come back to the kitchen in muddy boots to get a bowl to bale it out. My grandfather used a bleach bottle, cut just so, and the sound of it would scrape on the wooden boat as he tossed each leak back to sea.

The ORANGE HORSE

Once upon a time there was an orange horse in a field in Scotland. I remember its name was Fred. That's what the American called it. He wore cowboy boots. He came from Texas to work on the oil rigs. Whenever he wasn't at sea, he would go to the fence and hang his arms out and the horse would run to him from wherever it happened to be.

The TREES of MAYHEW PARK

That's his title. It's the only part we know. He never told anyone the rest. He works just off the Mount Baker Highway. On the other side of the fence are relics. Old words are stacked in rows like a grocery store. It takes a farmer to know where everything grows. If you need a part for a poem or a story, this is the place to go. Nothing is forgotten, nothing is without repair, the words you're looking for are here.

APPARENTLY a BIRD

Apparently there's a bird that causes insomnia. It likes to perch by a window early before dawn and it takes every stress, regret, undone worry, every woe that could possibly toss and stretch your conscience, each wish and wrong bend in memory, and it turns them into song. Sometimes it will sing for hours. You can't help but listen. The pharmacy sells a remedy. It comes in a little paper box to put on your sill. I don't know if it works.

BRASS FOOT

"I'm afraid your son has Brass Foot." The boy's parents stared at the sight of his trumpet-colored foot. "As for treatment…" the doctor shrugged, "I can't promise that we can reduce it to anything less than tin. Maybe zinc if we're lucky." The boy's father shook his head and sighed, "A zinc foot…" He dug into his pocket with his aluminum hand, found his pen to sign the necessary documents.

LUCKY

"Just keep telling me the winners," he said, "and we'll get that place in the country. Then you won't have to bend so low to fit in." He rustled the *Herald* racing form in front of his lucky pet's nose. "Take a look... Black Tie looks good, but don't let me cloud your vision. Just knock. You know the odds. You've never been wrong..." He leaned back to wait. Holes punched in the wall let in more light and air, traffic rush, flies. He waited. As soon as there was a reply, he could call his bookie. He scratched his hands. "No more city... Just meadows and sky..." The answer would take them there. Then it came. Effortlessly, the giraffe clapped its hoof against the floor. Once, twice, three times.

The LAKE ERIE HIGH SCHOOL MARCHING BAND

We were still asleep. It was a Saturday morning. It's so nice to forget about the alarm clock for a couple days a week. But all of a sudden there was a marching band on our street. Every loud brass and reed instrument, booming drums and snares. The sun was shining round the curtains. My hand hit that cloth and pushed it aside to see if Glenn Miller's crashed plane with all his orchestra had come back to blaring life.

BRING OUT BARBARA

There will be times you really need her. When that happens, you will know. I called the 1-800 number this week. The agent told me this would be my 3rd call. I didn't know you're only allowed 4 times. Luckily my wife is listed on our account and she hasn't used any yet. I don't know what we'd do without Barbara.

CHURCH MUSIC

When I lived in a brokenhearted palace in Seattle, I looked forward to Sunday morning. Even if it was raining—especially if it was raining, that would just add to the sound—I got by the open window and listened to the Baptist church. People were arriving like kings and queens in the parking lot. I could hear the heavenly music each time the door opened and closed.

The BRIGHT PUDDLE

After 25 days of rain, the sun finally returned with a crash. I ran outside to look and discovered it was an accident. A tanker truck had tipped on its side and sunshine was spilled all over the street. Birds were singing next to it. A girl in red rubber boots was laughing, jumping in and out of the bright puddle.

The COIN FACTORY

There's a sign by the register at The Dollar Store:

> Due to a national coin shortage
> exact change is appreciated on
> cash purchases when possible

I asked the teenaged cashier about it. He didn't know. He shrugged and said, "Maybe the coin factory shut down." I laughed, but it turned out he was right. Outside, I saw the *Herald* vending machine and I read the terrible headlines about the factory layoffs. Hundreds were out of work. How will all those people make their money?

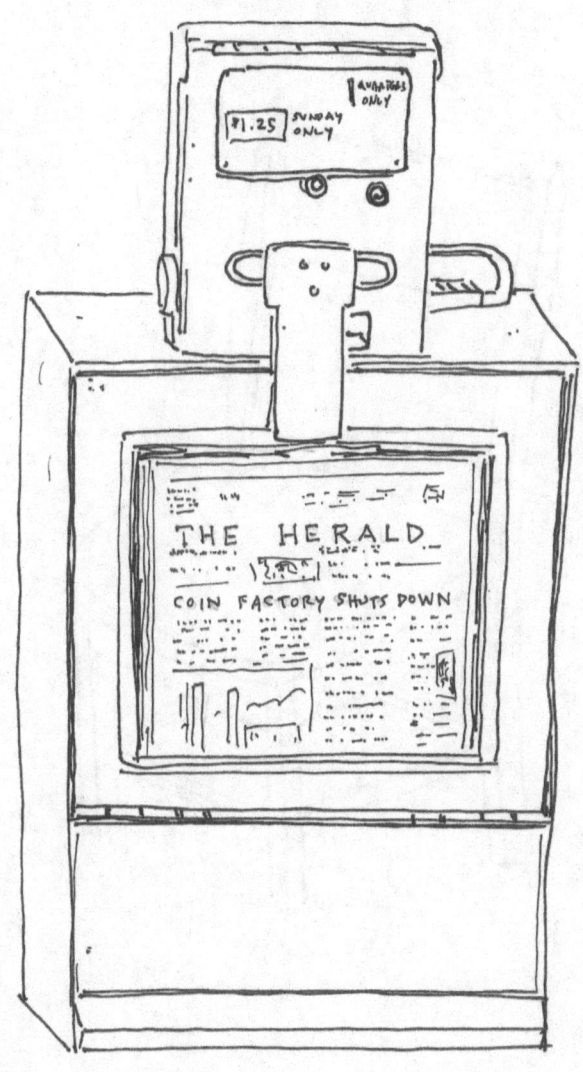

The LAUGH TRACK

The laugh track gave him trouble all day long. Everything he said ended with guffaws and applause. There was no way to stop it, it followed his words like a shadow. He wasn't trying to be funny either, he had never been anything but dour and glum. It was only by evening, after hours of side-splitting laughs, that he could he finally accept the proof and consider himself a comedian.

The HIDDEN RIVER

One summer I had a job putting shadows on windows. They came in slick rolls, heavy as night. They covered anything anyone with money didn't want you to look in and see. Mostly we would cut out pieces for expensive cars, but sometimes we went to mansions. Lots of window on those! That's when we would load the truck with rolls. It was sunny, we were up on the roof and I could see the inside of their house the way a bird would, and I saw what they had running across their floor. A flowing river, a bridge, plants from a Tarzan movie. It made you want what they had even if it meant hiding it from view.

1962

A curious survivor of the Seattle World's Fair had a room to itself, spread across the entire floor like a pond. It was an exact replica of Puget Sound, Lake Washington and all the waterways. A control panel connected to different parts. If you pressed a button for the Ballard Locks, a few drops of blue dye fell in and you could watch where the current went. It was more than a map though, it was a living being, one with water for blood, that only asked to be allowed to flow.

The ALLIGATOR BANK

I would dare myself to pull myself up and look over the edge at the still water and that's how I spotted all the money. Why did people go to the zoo and throw money at the alligator? Quarters and dimes shined like fish and tempted it to sink and crawl. Then what do you do with an alligator that's had its fill of coins? Shake it upside down? Turn its tail? They're not meant for that. Eventually the zoo put up a mesh wall, but there was a time you could lean over and like a bad penny fall right in.

LIFE in the INNERTUBE

Round and round, dizzy by it all, it's hard to grab the ground, why try? We go and go, and other people do it too—we catch glimpses of them rolling by. Downhill, bumped along, and sometimes, mercifully we slow, spin to a rest, rocked atop a circle of grass with daisies growing through.

The AUTHOR of WATER

D would go to the library every single day. He was a character there, like someone in their own poem. But his story was a mystery, just a few clues left behind, like the gallon jugs of water he would hide on every floor, leaving what little we know of him buried in the bookshelves.

The NEIGHBORS

All day long they went back and forth across McKenzie carrying boxes, clothes, kitchenware, furniture, rolling a piano across the tar. The breath of one house turning into the breath of the other. Their dogs passed one another pulling on leashes, up driveways, closing their doors as evening fell.

ASLEEP in OHIO

A baby stroller ride away from our Ohio rental house, down the clacking cement path by the road, onto Ontario, we would sing and talk and point out birds in yards. At Meeker Street we were close to sleep. It idled in the transformers, lay in the grass surrounding the power substation hum. That's where we stopped and counted rabbits. We made up names for them and gave them jobs they liked to do (tuning circuits, adjusting wires, checking levels and turning dials). We imagined their homes and families underground, where bunnies had their dinners, blew out candles and went to bed. Sure enough, one more yawn and we could turn around.

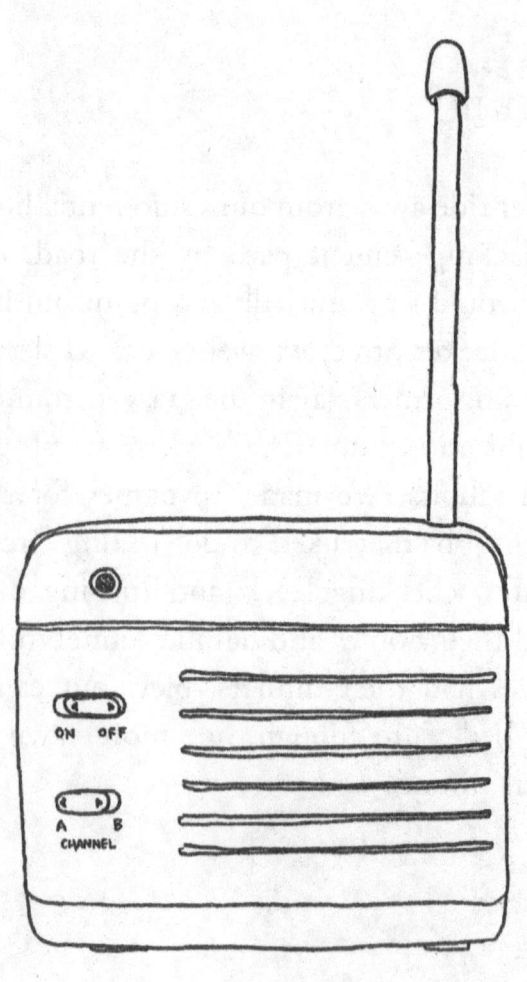

DREAM TELEGRAM

So happy to see you again. Missing years mean nothing. Sunshine not of this world. Come back here anytime. I'll be waiting.

The COWS of 32nd STREET

A neighbor who grew up here tells me about the cows and now I picture them. Memory makes another world. Where a car is parked beside the curb, I see a black and white cow looking through apartments that aren't there, where other cows are watching it from a field.

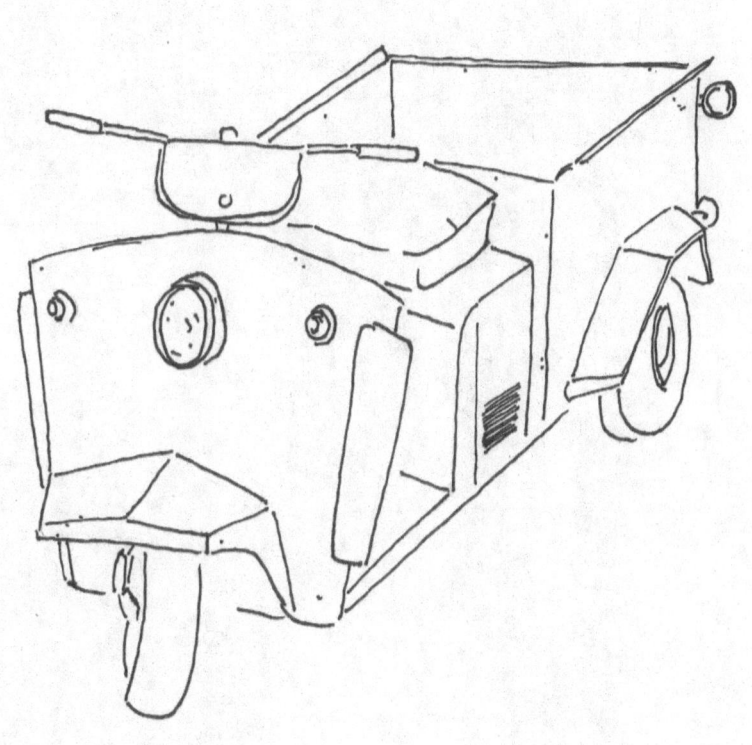

The MERMAID NEXT DOOR

We hear her splash. She likes her privacy. All you can see through the lattice is the green scales of her tail.

The ROBOT

The robot hasn't moved since summer. It's a long wait for that ice cream truck to come back, but a robot has nothing but time.

A GALLON of MILK

He had a job there for a little while, a dairy in the city of Portland. There weren't any cows, just aisles of cold storage, forklifts and pallets. We walked by the loading dock where he used to take his break, with his frozen hands stuffed in his pockets, alone because nobody would talk to him. They were all old guys who had been there for years and they could tell he wouldn't be around for long. A gallon of milk would start out warm and end up cold as snow.

SOMETHING TO TALK ABOUT

I'm aware of angels and other so-called miracles flying just out of reach. I don't know what they're doing. I suppose they're wondering the same thing about me. If we met it would give us something to talk about.

The FIELD

The wind blows the bare clarinet trees, the field is a frozen stage where all the weeds lay flat. My dog stops and points, paw held up. We both stare…We hear the bells on the children marching in a row from the daycare, only no, they're not…Only a blackberry hedge and a hundred yards separates us from the wobbly line of bundled up penguins coming our way.

The CHICKENS

On one side of 13th an outdoor pen holds seven chickens and right across the street, in another yard, are three more. There's not much space between them, maybe a hundred feet, but I don't think the chickens are aware of each other. The street could be the Atlantic Ocean. Or maybe they're just aloof.

# 4 BIRDS

The Beatles never left India. There are four birds. For fifty years, they've been singing, blended in with the flowers.

The VISIBLE WOMAN

We bought her in a box at a garage sale in Maine. She was mostly invisible: her skin was clear molded plastic. And you could see her heart. She held out her see-through hands like someone catching rain.

AMONG the SEAGULLS

Who would have thought I could down a whole tin of sardines and like it? That was one of my grandfather's treats. He would also walk with us on the beach, pick up a blue mussel shell and split it open with his knife. Then we all screamed as he ate that tidepool creature. I wonder if it's inevitable: how long will it be before you can find me on the flats, picking through seaweed with the gulls?

The VOICE of the SEA

The Malantic was torpedoed on March 9, 1943 and took an hour to sink in the North Atlantic. My grandfather told me how the fire spread like flowers on the surface, how he had to dive under that meadow looking for some wreckage to hold onto. The waves would have been urging him to let go. The ocean screamed and pulled. It took another hour for help to arrive. That night sat on his shelf for years, crowded into a bottle with a sailing ship, with all the water drained out and the voice of the sea gone quiet.

SOMETHING BRIGHT

We go back and forth between this world and dreams. By carriage or boat or motor car, the fare is paid in sunlight. That's something they crave. We carry it on us from our day. It clings to us like cobwebs. The taxi stops when I get there and when I give the driver something bright, I'm dropped off inside a house I know, in a world where I can fly.

The FOREST of the MOON

Fresh snow has quieted this world. We make the first footprints on it like astronauts leaving a trail from our rocket to the forest of the moon. In leaps and bounds we laugh as we run. Nothing here is lifeless, life is everywhere.

HER LITTLE FARM

In her apartment she has a goat, a chicken, and a talking crow. Oh, and a beehive by the window. Corn grows in flowerpots. At night, she can hear the barn owl behind the wall, hunting in the vast dark distance between the standing lamp and the kitchenette.

INSIDE

Coyote tracks led from the woods, around the pond to the edge of the house. That's where they walked up the white covered steps. The door left a pattern fanned across the snow when it opened and closed. Inside, hanging on the coatrack is a wet gray animal fur. It isn't cold inside. The chimney sends warm lazy smoke drifting into the trees.

SNOW HOTEL

Have you seen the brochure? The walls are made of snow and the windows are ice. Four stories tall, with balconies attached like whiskers. None of the radiators work. The janitor made sure the furnace stays broken. The bellhop is frozen against the counter. The keys chatter on the wall. They have a select clientele. Upstairs, a polar bear uses the phone to call for room service.

A CLASSIC

I was cutting thick slices of snow from the driveway, heaving them to the side, when a blind man appeared. I was glad I also shoveled the sidewalk. I heard his cane tap. He complimented my work and told me he had a joke. "Why couldn't the lifeguard save the hippie?" I thought of all the answers to that while he gleamed at me, until finally I said I don't know. "He was too far out!"

The ASH

The bus driver asked me what kind of tree it was. Usually I know things like that. Winter was an odd time to wonder, just a dark overcoat of bark, with all its leaves fallen off like a villain who had no fingerprints. I had to wait until spring, when it made its move, trying to steal the sun with a thousand greedy green hands.

The RIGHT CONDITIONS

I don't know why, but out of the blue I was thinking about *The Flying Nun* TV show. For some reason I believed Sally Field had magical powers to fly. After doing some research though, tracking down and reading the original paperback book, *The 15th Pelican*, I'm surprised to find that's not the case at all. Her ability was all scientific, based on weight and lift and aerodynamics. In other words, anyone can fly given the right conditions.

The BEGINNING

This doesn't begin with the beginning. It begins somewhere in the middle with the story already going. To know what happens in the beginning, we'll have to wait. Someone has misplaced it, but it will show up. Looking like someone coming down the stairs from a nap.

PUZZLES

They took him out of class and brought him to a room with a big table. He sat down and they opened the cardboard box in front of him. He started out doing wooden puzzles, then it was mazes, numbers, ink shapes on paper. After a while, they led him out of the room, back to class. They were talking about Christopher Columbus. He waited for recess. When the clock bell sputtered, everyone stood in line and went to the playground and he climbed the slide up to a cloud in the sky.

The SHELL

I work in a snail shell. We make the walls. It's not the greatest job I've had but it's not the worst. My boss is the reason I started looking for a different job. I won't go into that but suddenly one day she told us she was quitting. It was incredible. I already had an interview at a birdnest and now she was leaving…So I stuck around. Wall making isn't bad. The shell was growing and there's a future in walls. Over the next few days, we worked in a sort of rare air. We never felt like this here. We even played the radio. That all changed when the management brought in our new boss. Her son.

A RED LETTER DAY

One winter morning a few years back we were driving along the waterfront not far from the alphabet factory when we had to swerve the car. Letters were scattered in the road, fallen off some truck. It must have just happened. People were still reacting. I saw a man running down the hill with a big red J hooked over his shoulder.

The WORLD SERIES in HEAVEN

This isn't about Willie Mays wearing angel wings. The World Series was playing on the car radio when I drove into a dog. After that horrible thud and a yelp, I thought it was all over. But as I let go of the brake, the dog ran off towards the apartment building nearby. It hopped past a guy standing in the doorway. I called out to him, but he said it was okay, "That happens a lot." It was beaten down many times, but it always got back up.

A BITE of APPLE

A few weeks have gone since our dog died and I still go to the backyard to check on her, see that the snow is a blanket, and the blackberries are standing guard. She doesn't follow me back to the house, but every time I cut an apple, I think how she would be waiting for a bite.

A MOMENT with the MAP

Barking and carrying on like a dogsled, the geese slide across the sky. Any reins must be hopelessly tangled, they only guess where they're going by shouting directions at each other. It's too bad they dropped their map back at Burlington. A maid at the Holiday Inn found it, thought for a moment it was a lottery ticket before throwing it away.

The AMALGAMATED TRANSIT UNION

I don't know why I keep taking buses in dreams. I never get where I want to go. I end up bending the wrong way, staring out the window at an architecture of anthills. Then it always stops for me in some cemented part of a city I've never been. Like anyone caught in this situation, I'd be interested if the transit authority is any better in someone's else's mind. Maybe I just need to give the drivers a raise.

BETTY'S DOG

Betty's dog stands by the door and wags her tail. Her eyes are like marbles. She doesn't need them to know we're there. She leans a little against the other dog as they move backwards to let us inside. 1975 was her house in Massachusetts and the people who came and went, and dreams and days were all the same, seen without sight.

WHEN I WAS SUPERMAN

First of all, she was late. The night wind and rain shook the black windows. An empty wooden podium, some plastic chairs in a room curtained off from the cafeteria. Most people had already left. I waited. Then the glass door flung open and Margot Kidder blew through. She fought off the weather in a heavy wool coat, and her makeup had run. She apologized, she just flew in. Her speech for Jesse Jackson was rushed and then she was off to the airport again. I held the door for her.

A HOUSE on a STREET FULL of STARS

The moon is a house on a street full of stars. Nobody lives there now, the windows are boarded up and the door is nailed shut. You notice it, think of something, then you're on to other things. That's the way it is. The moon stays quiet, slowly pulling off a shadow until once a month it glows.

The DEER TAILOR

Footprints are sewn to the thin ice-covered pond. The tracks of a deer. It walked through the shallows early this morning, over to the ground rising on the other side where its thread continues, tailor stitched to the wind

KAREN WAGNER'S DOG

What happened to Karen Wagner's dog? It was a rescue that was a street dog for a year and a half. Living in a house made it nervous: the clean floor, carpets, the sigh of heating vents, food in a bowl, the TV and telephone. When it ran away, she called a detective, a guy in a plaid suit who drove all around town in a yellow car. She spoke to a reporter at the *Herald* and they ran a picture in the classifieds. Jobs, want ads, the horoscope. Where it's gone is right among us in the lost and found.

KING in a TAXI

I saw the cold get in a taxi and go. It was making the rounds, sitting in the backseat where the windows were opaque with ice. Sure, it can ride around town like a king, but it should know its days are numbered. The cab driver already removed his gloves.

The ORSON WELLES CINEMA

Night and the lights of Cambridge were candlewax splashes. Massachusetts is covered with water, slush on the street and the sidewalk leading to it. In those days there were rusty pipes laid underground. A skilled plumber could tap into one, Bergman, Fellini, or Ozu. Movies would gush out in a bright flame that had to be captured and tamed into a river of light. They had to be handled carefully, I once saw Jean Renoir catch on fire, melt to the screen like a pressed flower.

1911

The pond is cracking into a hundred ice photographs like this one: Boston Harbor when there was still a forest of sailing ship masts. The black coal smoke from the city blew them back and forth around the world. It's my grandfather's memory. He was born in 1911 and stamped by the sea. I held the photo until it melted from my hand.

The SNOW PHARAOH

He was mighty for a while, but today it's 44 degrees and sunny and the sound of running water flows like the Nile.

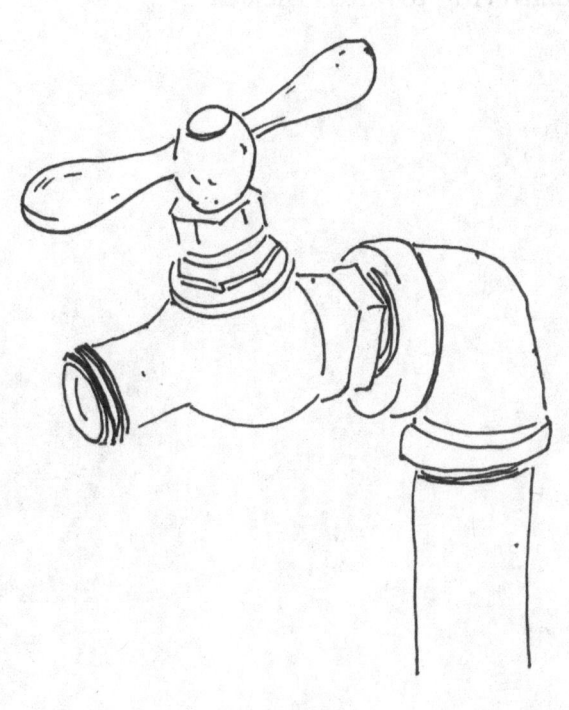

JUST MARRIED

Connelly Creek runs fast and full of cold electricity, speeding to meet Padden Creek and drive together like a Just Married car with tin cans tied to the bumper clattering towards the sea.

The 24th STREET RIVER

There are also smaller streams, ones that don't have names, or exciting beginnings and ends. They only appear after a hard rain or snowmelt, forming a trickle by the sidewalk, or lying shallow in the ditch on 24th Street. That's where someone poured out a teakettle filled with glass and watercress.

The MARTIAN MAILMAN RETURNS

The mail truck sat by the edge of the plain. The lights were turned off, the engine too. He didn't want to scare them off. First he saw their campfire. Then as he focused the binoculars, he counted five Martians around it. They weren't usually this close to the road. They lived out there beyond the hills and the bleak canals. He wondered what they were doing. He didn't want to leave, but he still had 500 miles to go.

The FREQUENCY of OTHER WORLDS

No longer the star he was, he is still known around the neighborhood. He drives to the bakery every week to get banana bread. He stands by the glass display case and waits for them to wrap it. When he goes home, he parks on gravel and gets out on a shadow. His house has an antenna a hundred feet tall. Wire rigging holds it down. It points straight up at the sky like a magic beanstalk and when he goes on the air, he can tune into the frequency of other worlds up there.

OHIO FAIRY TALE, part 1

There needs to be a fairy tale about it for the future children of Ohio. I only went to his house once. It was a long drive—you could easily fall asleep—past the farms shut down for winter. Snow grew in the fields. Route 13 turned into smaller roads and the car kept turning until it went into woods. Just when you had no idea where you were, that's where his house was. It was raining when we got out of the car. The sound came down through the trees.

OHIO FAIRY TALE, part 2

Only in a story would you see a Chinese restaurant in the woods. After the Ming Palace went broke, he bought every part and moved it all out here. Jade tiled roof, pillars with dragons, round red windows, and the big neon lettered sign. It made you hungry to look at: the thought of spring rolls, wontons, hot chow mein noodles, steamed rice, and chop suey. An old man lived alone inside. No that's not quite true, he had a slow-moving Siamese cat.

COMFORT

At night, the salmon can hear the rain on the roof. They're tired, their work is done, the sea is dark and it's a comfort to know that up above those layered waves, more water fills the air.

MISS MILLIPEDE

Open the door in the morning and she is bubbling next to you until she can slip through. Every day, rain or shine, you watch her run across the lawn, fast as a thousand legs.

10,000 SPRING FLOWERS

Two ducks on the pond. They stare suspiciously. No wonder. Underwater, one of them has a foot on the safe dial, turning it to the left, to the right, listening for that last click that will open the vault buried in the mud all winter long. Inside it is a treasure. 10,000 spring flowers, frogs, and a clutch of redwing blackbirds on tall cattails. Quite a haul for two ducks from Lake Whatcom.

A VICTIM of HELIUM

My wife said she was taking lessons on how to float in her dream last night. That's easy, I bragged, I've been doing that in my dreams since I was five. She was quick with her reply, "Then maybe you should stop."

A CUP of SUGAR

He's no bigger than a cup of sugar now. A crow caws at the car that just parked nearby. A *Herald* reporter carefully crosses the wet lawn. She figures there's bound to be some wisdom in the snowman's last words.

The FARMERS' ALMANAC PREDICTS

Spring will arrive in a month. It won't be an easy journey. We will have 3 more weeks of rain and wind, but occasional sunny days when you swear it's just around the corner. Be patient. When it gets here you'll know. The engine will hiss, the kids will jump off the roped stacks and already be playing when they hit the ground, trampling the daffodils.

A DISTANT BARK

I spread a packet of seeds around our dog cemetery stone and I pour a little water on the earth every day. Any flowers that grow will remind me of her. A poppy will lean towards me when I get near. Later, on a summer night I'll hear a distant columbine bark.

VIENNA CUCKOO CLOCK CLEANERS

They're located on Magnolia Street, just a block from the bus station. Open the door and right away you're greeted by an orchestra of tick-tocking clocks, suspended from the ceiling track like clean laundry. This is where time is taken care of, steamed, pressed like musical notes into a player piano eternally unrolling.

A BLUE OCTOPUS

On another planet or a cartoon universe, they have a streetsweeper too. You hear the rumble for half a block as it nears. The birds of the neighborhood flee in front. Next door it sounds like a three-headed dog is warning us. Then it appears. A steam-driven wheelbarrow steered by a blue octopus, clearing the pavement with a dustpan and broom.

The FRIENDLY GIANT

The Friendly Giant had a castle I went to every morning when I was one. The music would play, he would let down the drawbridge and open the doors. An imaginary world as unreal as California seems to me now, animals, songs, something to laugh about, until it was time to say goodbye. Then the doors and the drawbridge would close, and the castle would turn into sky. I was only beginning to see every day starting and ending the same way.

1973

There were a lot of flowers in those days. It meant something to have them next to the TV, on the kitchen tablecloth, stuck in milk bottles, or dried on windowsills. There were games with buttercups and dandelions. A girl with flowers in her hair walking by was a song you already knew the lyrics to.

The SEA VISITOR, part 1

The tide is low, showing the flats and mats of seaweed that carpet the underwater floor. When the sea is gone it leaves all its clutter everywhere. I like to see what I can find. Shells and bits of colored glass fill my hand. I go past them with muddy shoes to where the last big rock is parked, sunk like a Pontiac. I stand on the dented, barnacle roof and look over the edge into the deep green emerald start of the Pacific Ocean.

The SEA VISITOR, part 2

I think a submarine could come pop up right beside me and I wouldn't mind. I would wait for the crew to unscrew the hatch and I might go with them on some adventure under icebergs and sunsets to a jungle island full of dinosaurs. Amazing places I can only visit with crayons. Or maybe this rock itself will let me climb inside and I can look out windows like someone in the backseat of a car watching a rainy day.

The SEA VISITOR, part 3

That's when I see somebody else in my reflection below. Two eyes set in a gray ghost-like blur. A couple bubbles lift it closer to the surface and then a seal appears, close enough for me to reach and pet. I think of feeding it (we have some fish at home) and caring for it, being its friend, and I can put it in a wagon and bring it to school, or the swimming pool. I'm so excited thinking about the things we will do together, I don't have time to say goodbye.

1934

ZaSu Pitts just crashed in the backyard. She climbed out of the plane a little frail, but now she's sitting down in the living room in a flowered chair, no worse for the wear.

RHUBARB RADIO

The tulips are coming up again. They will let all the other flowers know; they will tell it on the radio. Right now their music is faint, only the cobweb of a song, like the drone you hear in the background of a supermarket, played for a vegetable audience.

The OTHER HOUSE

Avocado trees. A porch with a rocking chair. Two. I can picture it, can you?

UNDERGROUND and in the WIND

I went down the steps into there not knowing. I was only my son's age now, in a brick room underground, and as I spoke to the owner, he held a stack of records for me, fanned out like Tarot cards, and my fortune was Bud Powell. I carried that home. When it played, a whole other sound surrounded me and got stuck in the air above me like windchimes on the branch of a tree.

ROOSTER FISH

I took my lunch at a café a block away from work. We were living in Ohio then, where there were different birds like the cardinal, and there weren't any salmon as far as I knew. They had walleyes and bluegill and raccoon perch. The weirdest one appeared on the menu one day. I asked the waitress about it. She told me it came with a side order of soup.

An ASTRONAUT PARADE

The Return of Johnson Dracula almost happened. The scriptwriter had that heroic 1950s devotion to duty that put a man into outer space, and he pounded out a story in a month and took a cab to the studio when he was done. That's where he remembered how he put the script on the taxi roof when he got in. It was a three dollar fare. By then the pages were blowing all over town.

A BETTER, MORE PEACEFUL WORLD

A large moth knocked on the door today. I could see his antennas and fedora through the little window, but I opened the door anyway. What the hell. Let me tell you, there's no way to prepare yourself for the sight of a 6-foot moth in brown suit trying to hand you a brochure about a better, more peaceful world.

The INVISIBLE WOMAN

When our son was one, we watched *The Invisible Woman*. He stood with an arm on the table near the TV very seriously as he watched her unravel herself into thin air. It might have been the first time he considered an invisible person, that cups and saucers could seem to float by themselves.

The DREAM BIRD

It's twilight in a desert and I'm watching the dream bird. Back and forth, back and forth in the sky. When I know it isn't a real bird and I'm not really where it seems I am, the dream bird has done its job. It was the last thing I saw before I woke up here.

The TRICYCLE MIRACLE

Suddenly I hear a robin. After all these dark mornings, sound is returning! Listen…like a squeaky tricycle it pedals and waits, then starts again, turning a wheel that pulls at a sleeping sun.

BEFORE WORDS

Without a word of warning, the cherry tree has begun to blossom. It didn't notify the *Herald*. They have matters of the world to worry about. It didn't apply for a license downtown either. These things are beyond our workings. This has been happening long before words. A branch with pink flowers hovers over the fence.

CRABGRASS

I took our puppy for a walk in the woods. She was sniffing the air, standing on her back legs, pulling on the leash like a fairground ride, sure something was ahead of us. I know what it is: Spring. When I let her go in the field, she took off after that ball of bright light. It was warm as a sun, bouncing up the path with her running after. Every time it touched the ground, it left a green splash in the crabgrass.

SPRING EQUINOX

He is running through the woods and onto the sidewalk. Does he know he's being followed by a girl riding a bicycle, soft looking cheeks made rosy by the early morning air?

The ONE with the PICKET FENCE SMILE

The one with the picket fence smile stands on a lawn holding flowers for you.

SOMETHING BRIGHT

Writing & Drawings: Allen Frost

Written January—March 2021

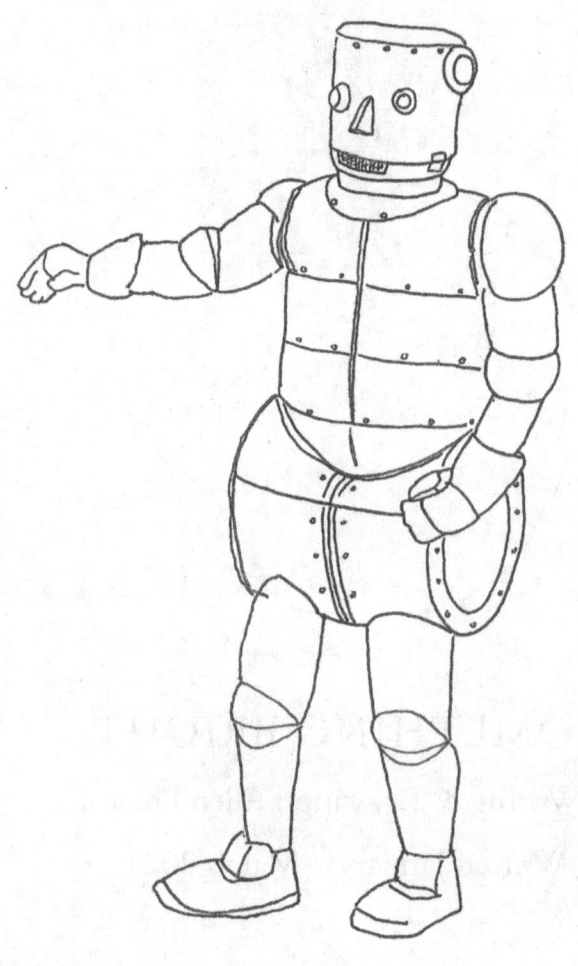

Illustration from *King Leopold's Slow Leak* (2000)

Books by Good Deed Rain

Saint Lemonade, Allen Frost, 2014. Two novels illustrated by the author in the manner of the old Big Little Books.

Playground, Allen Frost, 2014. Poems collected from seven years of chapbooks.

Roosevelt, Allen Frost, 2015. A Pacific Northwest novel set in July, 1942, when a boy and a girl search for a missing elephant. Illustrated throughout by Fred Sodt.

5 Novels, Allen Frost, 2015. Novels written over five years, featuring circus giants, clockwork animals, detectives and time travelers.

The Sylvan Moore Show, Allen Frost, 2015. A short story omnibus of 193 stories written over 30 years.

Town in a Cloud, Allen Frost, 2015. A three part book of poetry, written during the Bellingham rainy seasons of fall, winter, and spring.

A Flutter of Birds Passing Through Heaven: A Tribute to Robert Sund, 2016. Edited by Allen Frost and Paul Piper. The story of a legendary Ish River poet & artist.

At the Edge of America, Allen Frost, 2016. Two novels in one book blend time travel in a mythical poetic America.

Lake Erie Submarine, Allen Frost, 2016. A two week vacation in Ohio inspired these poems, illustrated by the author.

and Light, Paul Piper, 2016. Poetry written over three years. Illustrated with watercolors by Penny Piper.

The Book of Ticks, Allen Frost, 2017. A giant collection of 8 mysterious adventures featuring Phil Ticks. Illustrated throughout by Aaron Gunderson.

I Can Only Imagine, Allen Frost, 2017. Five adventures of love and heartbreak dreamed in an imaginary world. Cover & color illustrations by Annabelle Barrett.

The Orphanage of Abandoned Teenagers, Allen Frost, 2017. A fictional guide for teens and their parents. Illustrated by the author.

In the Valley of Mystic Light: An Oral History of the Skagit Valley Arts Scene, 2017. A comprehensive illustrated tribute. Edited by Claire Swedberg & Rita Hupy.

Different Planet, Allen Frost, 2017. Four science fiction adventures: reincarnation, robots, talking animals, outer space and clones. Cover & illustrations by Laura Vasyutynska.

Go with the Flow: A Tribute to Clyde Sanborn, 2018. Edited by Allen Frost. The life and art of a timeless river poet. In beautiful living color!

Homeless Sutra, Allen Frost, 2018. Four stories: Sylvan Moore, a flying monk, a water salesman, and a guardian rabbit.

The Lake Walker, Allen Frost 2018. A little novel set in black and white like one of those old European movies about death and life.

A Hundred Dreams Ago, Allen Frost, 2018. A winter book of poetry and prose. Illustrated by Aaron Gunderson.

Almost Animals, Allen Frost, 2018. A collection of linked stories, thinking about what makes us animals.

The Robotic Age, Allen Frost, 2018. A vaudeville magician and his faithful robot track down ghosts. Illustrated throughout by Aaron Gunderson.

Kennedy, Allen Frost, 2018. This sequel to Roosevelt is a coming-of-age fable set during two weeks in 1962 in a mythical Kennedyland. Illustrated throughout by Fred Sodt.

Fable, Allen Frost, 2018. There's something going on in this country and I can best relate it in fable: the parable of the rabbits, a bedtime story, and the diary of our trip to Ohio.

Elbows & Knees: Essays & Plays, Allen Frost, 2018. A thrilling collection of writing about some of my favorite subjects, from B-movies to Brautigan.

The Last Paper Stars, Allen Frost 2019. A trip back in time to the 20 year old mind of Frankenstein, and two other worlds of the future.

Walt Amherst is Awake, Allen Frost, 2019. The dreamlife of an office worker. Illustrated throughout by Aaron Gunderson.

When You Smile You Let in Light, Allen Frost, 2019. An atomic love story written by a 23 year old.

Pinocchio in America, Allen Frost, 2019. After 82 years buried underground, Pinocchio returns to life behind a car repair shop in America.

Taking Her Sides on Immortality, Robert Huff, 2019. The long awaited poetry collection from a local, nationally renowned master of words.

Florida, Allen Frost, 2019. Three days in Florida turned into a book of sunshine inspired stories.

Blue Anthem Wailing, Allen Frost, 2019. My first novel written in college is an apocalyptic, Old Testament race through American shadows while Amelia Earhart flies overhead.

The Welfare Office, Allen Frost, 2019. The animals go in and out of the office, leaving these stories as footprints.

Island Air, Allen Frost, 2019. A detective novel featuring haiku, a lost library book and streetsongs.

Imaginary Someone, Allen Frost, 2020. A fictional memoir featuring 45 years of inspirations and obstacles in the life of a writer.

Violet of the Silent Movies, Allen Frost, 2020. A collection of starry-eyed short story poems, illustrated by the author.

The Tin Can Telephone, Allen Frost, 2020. A childhood memory novel set in 1975 Seattle, illustrated by author like a coloring book.

Heaven Crayon, Allen Frost, 2020. How the author's first book Ohio Trio would look if printed as a Big Little Book. Illustrated by the author.

Old Salt, Allen Frost, 2020. Authors of a fake novel get chased by tigers. Illustrations by the author.

A Field of Cabbages, Allen Frost, 2020. The sequel to The Robotic Age finds our heroes in a race against time to save Sunny Jim's ghost. Illustrated by Aaron Gunderson.

River Road, Allen Frost, 2020. A paperboy delivers the news to a ghost town. Illustrated by the author.

The Puttering Marvel, Allen Frost, 2021. Eleven short stories with illustrations by the author.

Something Bright, Allen Frost, 2021. 106 short story poems walking with you from winter into spring. Illustrated by the author.

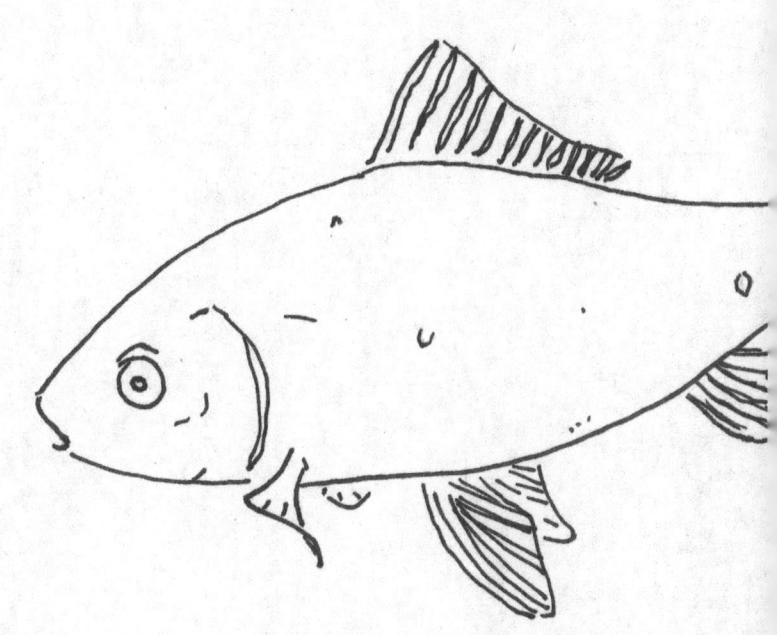

www.ingramcontent.com/pod-product-compliance
Lightning Source LLC
LaVergne TN
LVHW031540060526
838200LV00056B/4591